RIPS IN THE ETHER

Tales of the Ravensdaughter
- Adventure Four

Erin Hunt Rado

Copyright © 2022 Erin Hunt Rado

All rights reserved

The characters and events portrayed in this book are fictitious. Any similarity to real persons, living or dead, is coincidental and not intended by the author.

No part of this book may be reproduced, or stored in a retrieval system, or transmitted in any form or by any means, electronic, mechanical, photocopying, recording, or otherwise, without express written permission of the publisher.

ISBN-13: 9798353703259

Cover design by: Erin Hunt Rado
Printed in the United States of America

For my beloved Paul

The Realme will ne're forsake them
These Walkers who defend
The king and queen below
For whom they make their stand.

Trusted by their masters
A Walker will not fail.
Honored by their masters
They welcome duty's call.

- from the Scrolls of Imari

Alerice looked up at a dawn sky of pale blue green. The clouds were an opalescent mix of white, pink, and gold. A light breeze caressed her cheeks as it played in her blonde hair.

She and Kreston had taken their leisure on an oak-topped hill overlooking a sight Alerice had sometimes tried to picture, but never thought she would see – the Royal Range. It stood in the distance, its thin, snow-covered peaks scraping the sky like jagged teeth. As with the clouds, the impending sunrise had cast their caps in pinks and pale yellows, and Alerice awaited the moment when the sunlight would strike them.

Kreston had said that this was a sight few people ever beheld. The time of day and the time of year needed to be just right for the most grandiose effect. Fortunately, after leaving the traveler's rest and riding for a day and night, he had guided them to the perfect spot. Even though she knew she had broken his heart by retaking the Raven Queen's armor, she could not deny his company.

He had said very little as they rode, and she had done likewise. Captain had kept pace with Jerome, even though Jerome was a Realme pony and capable of covering greater distances.

There hadn't been any need to hunt for dinner, for the denizens of the traveler's rest had been so grateful to be rid of Belmaine, Goddess of Passion and Chaos, that they had stuffed both their saddlebags with meats and cheeses, and even a few treats.

Alerice had asked for both water and ale so that she could dilute her cup after she and Kreston had stopped to camp. She was a tavern mistress, after all, and knew the advantage of drinking only half of what others drank.

Strangely, she had not felt the need to sleep. Nor had Kreston, which Alerice found odd considering all the physical exertion it had taken to dispel the goddess. Kreston had explained that increased stamina was a gift to Realme Walkers, and Alerice was obviously on track to living up to her birthright.

Still, they had sipped through the night and now enjoyed the morning as the campfire dwindled down to embers.

"So, I've been meaning to ask," Kreston said. "Your old tavern was called the Cup and Quill?"

"Um hmmm," Alerice said inside her cup.

"That's a strange name," he said. "Usually tavern names are stronger, like the White Hound or the Three Lions, or something."

Alerice shrugged. "It was Uncle Judd's name. The 'Cup' part was simple. It was a tavern, after all. I think he chose the 'Quill' because he loved writing poetry. He was actually good at it. I've seen some of the love letters he wrote to Aunt Carol when they were courting."

"Hmmm," Kreston commented, taking a bite of cheese before chasing it with a drink.

"The tavern's name was fun, though," Alerice continued. "Every so often we would have a contest.

The person who wrote me the best love poem would win a free ale."

"Love poems, huh? You collected lovers in Navre?"

Alerice hid a blush. "No. And I wasn't looking for any, but when you have a, what did you call me once? Oh yes, a 'handsome woman' running a bar, and you have gents willing to abase themselves to win a free drink, well it was a unique way of promoting the establishment.

"And it worked fairly well. One of our poets wound up in the court of the Prime Cheval, Lord Andoni. Two others, I heard, went to Navre's sister city, A'Leon, and joined the court of its Cheval, Lord Bolivar."

"Sounds like the Cup and Quill was quite a place."

"It was, Kreston," she said with a recollecting smile. "I had many happy moments there."

Alerice could not help but drift off into nostalgia even as the sky grew brighter in the throes of the advancing sunrise. However, she could sense Kreston watching her, which he made known by clearing his throat to attract her attention. Then he drew a breath and recited.

"Upon the shore I think of thee.
Your eyes that dance with starlight,
Your hair caught in the moonlight,
Your lips I long to kiss.

Why did I e'er leave thee?
Your gentle, soft embrace,

The curve of your fair face,
Your heart that beats with mine.

No more again I'll see thee.
To battle I must go,
But please, love, this do know,
I'll cherish no one else."

"Kreston," Alerice exhaled. "A free drink to you, sir."

He smiled to himself. "I wrote it for a girl, Michelle. She was..." He tapped his fingers on his stomach. "She was something special."

Alerice smiled and then teased, "I imagine that through your years you've known several women, Captain."

"Alerice, if it's all the same, please don't call me that. And yes, I've known women. She was the one I wanted, though."

"And you had to leave her. Do you know what happened to her?"

"Nope, and I didn't try to find out. Hopefully, she got married to a good man and had a good life. She deserved a good life," Kreston said with a little shrug.

"I know you're going to say that you don't."

"Let's just enjoy the morning, Alerice. It's going to be our last."

"Well, that's a sad thought."

"Reality is rarely a happy thought." He turned on his hip to face her. "But you serve *her*, and I serve him, and that makes us rivals. I can never trust you now, and you can never trust me. If they fight, we fight, and that's an end to it."

"I don't think she would ever order me to attack you."

"You don't know her."

"True, but the last time, she released me rather than forced me to act against my will. She knows I could never kill you."

He humphed a little laugh. "You couldn't kill me if you tried, but that's not the point. She still might try to use you against me, which is to say against her husband."

"Why do those two fight so much?"

"It's just who they are. It's who they'll always be. They're eternal. We're merely dots. Oh, turn around."

Alerice did as he instructed just as the sunlight crested the horizon opposite the Royal Range, and the tops of the jagged peaks turned fine gold. As though ladled with molten metal, the sunlight poured down the mountain sides to coat every surface, and Alerice's breath drew up as she watched the natural wonder play out before her eyes.

Kreston stood and came up behind her. She stood as well, and he advanced until he was at her back. She could feel his warmth, and she knew that he wanted to press against her. She held her place to see what he would do, but all he allowed himself was to touch a lock of her hair and move it off of her armored shoulder. Then he petted it flat with the palm of his hand, tensed, and stepped to her side.

"I..." he said, a quiver in his voice. He cleared his throat again and continued. "I told you it was a sight to see."

"It is, Kreston," she said, not turning to him. "Thank you."

"Don't mention it. Just give thanks to Sukaar, Father God of Fire, for the day. He lives in those mountains, and we must all bow to him when beholding his home as it's kissed by the dawn."

Alerice closed her eyes and offered Father Fire a short prayer. Then she sensed something and looked aside, away from Kreston.

The maiden Oddwyn stood near an oak trunk, petting Jerome. Alerice glanced back at Kreston, who was moving over to his spot at the campfire. Then she looked again at Oddwyn.

"I know Oddwyn's here," Kreston said, not looking up as he attended to his gear. "*She* obviously needs you."

Alerice said nothing further as she collected her things and headed in Oddwyn's direction.

Kreston did his best to avert his eyes as he saw Alerice and Oddwyn converse. He began rolling up his blanket and preparing his kit, but then he felt the brand of the King of Shadows pulse upon his brow. A shiver shot through him, and he gulped down his reaction so that he could summon that familiar ice into his veins.

"*Come below, Kreston,*" the king said in his mind.

Kreston closed his hazel eyes and muttered aloud, "Yes, My King."

***

"You have alerted me to something dire, Alerice," the Raven Queen said in her voice of dark honey.

"My Queen?" Alerice replied as she stood in the queen's Twilight Grotto. The six tree branch-framed windowpanes displayed scenes of the Realme, one in particular being a field of flowers with blooms that glowed in rhythmic patterns.

However, the 'sky' above the blooms seemed troubled. It pushed and pulled against itself. Alerice tried to liken it to storm clouds gathering at a rapid speed, but the comparison did not seem right. The atmosphere seemed to bulge here and there as though it might rupture at any moment.

The Raven Queen had extended her willow-white hands toward the windowpane in order to align her essence with the fluctuations. Before her floated her gray orb, the interior of which swirled as though made of churning mist. The queen placed her palm over the orb to draw from its energy. As its swirling intensified, it emitted a grayish glow, and the queen directed its power toward the window.

The Raven Queen forced the orb's essence into the palpitating atmosphere. Alerice could see that the effort strained her, and she wanted to offer aid. However, she doubted that there was anything she could do.

Alerice watched the queen close her amethyst eyes as she exerted a significant amount of supernatural force. The atmosphere above the glowing flowers resisted her, and Alerice could feel the strain of their willful struggle. In the end the Raven Queen mastered the moment, and the 'sky' calmed into a steady hue of deep teal.

The queen exhaled and pressed her willow-white hands over her breast. The sleek feathers of her gown radiated their colors of black, purple, and emerald as the mistress of the Evherealme centered herself. Several moments passed, but eventually she recovered and stood tall. Then she turned and regarded Alerice.

"What you have just witnessed was an impending rip in the ether of the Realme," she stated.

"Yes, My Queen," Alerice replied.

The Raven Queen drew and released a thin breath, and then regarded her other windowpanes for any sign of danger.

"Upon occasion, outside pressures build upon the Realme's borders. When this occurs, a breach will try to form an abscess in our world. Anything may enter through this abscess, souls or creatures from other worlds. I have no idea what will transpire when it occurs.

"With my Eye," she said, gesturing to her gray orb, "I keep watch over the Realme. With my Eye, I can identify all breaches, as I did when sending you to Mortalia to deal with Prince Vygar. With my Eye, I can seal many rips before they abscess, as you have just seen, but the entrance of Belmaine into Mortalia was a breach I did not see, and this has given me cause for concern.

"If breaches open unbeknownst to me, then the Realme will become infected. I must bolster it against each breach, or else lance the breach and face the consequences of what will enter. I am more alert to the crisis now that you have shown me proof of Belmaine's infection above, and I have detected more potential abscesses than I am capable of managing.

"It is time to put you forward, my Ravensdaughter. It is time for you to go into battle to defend the Evherealme."

Go into battle, Alerice found herself repeating in her mind. She could not deny smiling at the thought.

***

The King of Shadows paced within his Hall of Misted Mirrors. A dozen elongated panes of varying sizes and shapes hung suspended in smokey tendrils. All were inert, save for the king's favorite, a large pane of black glass bordered in the same crystalline trim that adorned his long, open robe. A crown of dark crystals topped the pane to match his own crystal crown. Longer crystals jutted out from the top sides of the pane, matching the crystals which capped his pauldrons.

"Did you see what she did?" the King of Shadows asked as the pane relinquished the image of the field of glowing flowers and the nearly ruptured 'sky'.

"I did, My King," Kreston said as he stood at attention, his expression void as he stared 'eyes forward'.

"That damned Eye of hers," the king complained. "She used that damned Eye. Souls waited on the other side of that rupture, Kreston. My souls. Do you think Prince Vygar has been the only one in Mortalia collecting them for me? Now I must derive another way to import them. I will consume them in any manner I choose, regardless of what the queen thinks. Do you hear me, Captain?"

"I do, My King," Kreston said. He was well-accustomed to the frustrated rants of superior officers, which was why he used the physical focus of 'eyes forward' to create a semi-meditative state that allowed him to absorb information while rendering no outward appearance of cogent thought.

The King of Shadows regarded him, and paused to look him over. Then he scoffed, and yet admitted, "You are still the best mortal to wield my blade, Dühalde. Of all the men I have taken into my service, you have been the most successful, and why shouldn't you be? You are a born Walker, a rare find. But you were also a man of battle. When I sent you to war, you killed with great acclaim.

"The Ghost of the Crimson Brigade, they called you, a specter who stalked the ranks and slaughtered anyone. You haunted the thoughts of all fighting men, or at least you did before my wife got her hands on you."

Kreston did not react.

"Be that as it may," the king continued. "It's my wife's gem that is the problem. The Queen's Eye, she calls it. She claims that it was made from the amalgam of willing souls, but those souls were never willing. She took them when she measured them, plucking them like prizes. Some of those souls were mine, and I want my tally before she assigns any more to their resting places. Do you know how difficult it is to harvest them once they settle?

"The only souls I may enjoy for my own pleasure are the ones you claim in battle or the ones she does not know about or the, which is why I want you to fetch her Eye for me. And I don't want any excuse about not being able to look at her. I know you cannot. If you so much as glance at her, you will fall into madness, and we both know how long it takes you to recover. So, use the girl, Captain. You have no difficulty tolerating her presence, correct?"

"None, My King," Kreston said, arching his shoulders a bit further back. "I will do as you command."

"Of course you will," the King of Shadows said. "Now, let's set the stage for a plausible encounter so the girl might still trust you."

Kreston locked his jaw, unable to hide a blink that was slightly longer than normal.

***

"Oddwyn, this place is beautiful," Alerice said, looking about at a landscape that could only be found in dreams. The sky was magenta and bore off-white star clusters that brightened the canopy above in gradient tones so that some areas appeared lighter than others. The clusters swirled as though stirred by ethereal currents, making the landscape seem alive as brightness congealed briefly in one place before moving about to another.

The topography resembled a flow of light gray stone that Alerice swore must have been molten at some point. How else could it have pooled in gentle cascades before it had hardened? The stone's composure bore the same shimmer as the arches in the Convergence, which made her wonder if it contained bits of the white metal composing the Raven Queen's crown.

The flows stretched as far as Alerice could see, and they glistened whenever the star clusters congregated overhead. The stone also reflected the sky's magenta, so it appeared pinkish in places. It was rough terrain, not soft or dusty, and Alerice's boot soles were able to grip it, allowing her to feel sure of her footing.

"It is nice, yes," the youthful Oddwyn said, looking about the landscape he had likely seen hundreds of times. "I've watched the queen change the color of the sky too. Sometimes this place becomes more purple, sometimes more blue."

"It's a good thing that the folk above fear death," Alerice commented. "If they knew how breathtaking the Realme was, they'd never want to live their lives."

"It's because they do live them that the Realme exists. It is due to the collected consciousness of mortals that the Realme has been able to craft itself in so many ways. This is one of the prettier ways, but don't be fooled, Alerice. There are many baleful places within the Realme."

"Hmmm," Alerice said as she continued to stare at the magenta landscape. "I'll try to remember that."

"Do," Oddwyn said as he adjusted the iridescent chain that he had wrapped about his silvery scale mail tunic.

Alerice regarded him, noting that he wore the same armor that he had as a maiden during battle at the traveler's rest.

"No woman of war this time?" she asked.

"Naw," Oddwyn said with a backward shoulder rotation and a slight side-to-side head toss. "I feel like scruffing it up this time. Got your poles?"

Alerice eagerly presented her pixie pole cylinders and caused the blades to pop out as she stood on her guard.

"Yep," she said.

"Good," Oddwyn replied, observing her look of determination. Then he regarded her stance, adjusted it a bit, and though she gave him a look of 'What are you doing?' he reached up and flicked his finger against the Raven Queen's mark upon her brow.

She shook off the flick and half-glared at him, but her mark began to glow, and she could feel the queen's essence flowing through her. Oddwyn then looked over his shoulder at the two Raven Knights, and next at Ketabuck, the faun chief who had brought forth a cadre of his best warriors.

"We're ready, Your Majesty!" Oddwyn called out to the stars above. He then let loose a great whoop, and as the fauns bugled in reply, Alerice found herself cheering as well.

In her Twilight Grotto, the Raven Queen had expanded the vision of the magenta landscape so that it flowed over each of her six branch-framed panes.

She stood stoically as she commanded her Eye to appear above her left palm, and then floated her right hand over it as though stroking it. The swirls within began to churn easily at first, but with another pass of her hand, they swirled more dynamically until the Eye gave off a gray glow. The Raven Queen held the Eye before the central pane, and said, "I open this rip in the ether of the Evherealme."

The queen's words rang out against the magenta sky, churning the star clusters. "Dispatch whatever enters so that I may mend and seal the breach."

Oddwyn leaned in to Alerice.

"You know 'dispatch' means to kill, right?"

"Oddwyn," she said, not taking her eyes off the

stars. "Would this be a good time to tell you to shut up?"

"Probably," he said.

"Good, then shut up."

A flash tore across the magenta atmosphere, slicing through the star clusters and ripping open a long fissure.

The souls of mortals flew in as might clusters of leaves stirred up in a gale. Yet, while they filtered aimlessly above only to dissipate in batches, tension permeated the company as the atmosphere grew dense.

The landscape seemed to condense. Alerice looked about. She could see that the fissure created a rift through which the essence of the Realme and the essence of whatever world lay beyond exchanged some sort of balance, much the same way that air rises in a heated paper box. Only this pressure balance occurred in the reverse, with the Realme taking in the other world's essence rather than releasing its own to the other side.

Suddenly, oblong shapes appeared within the star clusters, buoyant for only a brief moment before they fell down to the pooled stone ground in a mass of heavy thuds.

Alerice watched the oblongs take shape, only to become brilliant green-yellow lizards, much longer than she was tall. One shook its head to clear its senses, and when the black slit pupils of its bright yellow eyes focused on her, it opened its jaws and hissed so loudly that Alerice thought she was back in Uncle Judd's brewery where a kettle was about to explode.

The beast roared at her and charged, its gait a waddle so quick that Alerice barely had time to jump toward it. She ran across its back and did her best to dodge its thrashing tail as she jumped off its flank.

Each of the oblongs took on the same lizard countenance, and the battle joined as Oddwyn loosed his iridescent chain. The Raven Knights took flight, and the fauns bugled again as they charged.

Alerice turned about and faced off against her lizard. The beast moved quickly, but she struck its jaw as it snapped at her. She sliced its forearms as it clawed for her. Dodging the tail was the most difficult feat, for it whipped in every direction.

Slaying Prince Vygar as a giant wolf had been easier, for then Alerice had been able to put out his eyes. She could not quite strike the eyes of this beast, for they were set too low and she would be within range of its claws. However, she did begin to feel the natural motion of her pixie poles guiding her as she swung one, primed the second, and then swung the second as she re-primed the first.

The lizard hissed again and prepared to charge, but Oddwyn's iridescent chain suddenly wrapped about its jaws to muzzle them shut.

"Kill it!" Oddwyn cried as he pulled on the chain with all his might.

Alerice lunged forward and sliced both poles deeply into the lizard's neck to splay it open. Its bluish blood poured out. She looked at it, then looked up to see Oddwyn leap over the lizard's back and then lunge forward to tackle and roll with her.

"Get clear!" he cried.

As they came to a stop and Oddwyn jumped away, he looked down at Alerice, who sat on the glimmering pooled stone.

"Its blood is acid. Don't let it touch you."

"Blood. Acid. Got it," Alerice said, as she jumped back to her feet and charged at another lizard.

The Raven Queen stood unmoving within her Twilight Grotto. Her Eye floated above her palm while her right hand extended to her central pane. Her amethyst eyes were open and fixed on the scene before her as she felt the abscess above drain dry.

Emptied of its infectious contents, she bent her mind to the task of sealing it.

The Raven Knights attacked the lizards with two-handed great swords. The fauns attacked with their razor-sharp prongs followed by both blunt force and edged weaponry. Oddwyn lashed out so precisely with his chain that he was able to blind several lizards so that Alerice could leap from one to another and slay them.

Alerice looked up to see the magenta sky further contract as the star clusters swarmed about the fissure to stitch it closed. She thought for a moment that the landscape might implode upon itself, for it had condensed a significant degree. She had no idea how she might escape if it did implode, so her only option was to keep fighting.

Suddenly a lizard hissed and reared up behind her. Alerice turned, ready for action, but a broadsword's point erupted from its chest, and Alerice had barely enough time to dodge the splatter of its acidic blue blood.

The beast's tongue lolled from its toothy jaws, and its head flopped aside as it fell forward, revealing Kreston and the king's two Shadow Warriors.

"Kreston!" she called.

He did not respond as he snapped for the Shadow Warriors to disperse and attack. Then he held his hand high overhead, and the King of Shadows' broadsword reappeared in his grip. He snarled as he hurled it at her head where it *whizzed* past her ear so closely that it stirred her hair.

Alerice looked over her shoulder to see the sword impale another lizard that had been about to charge. She looked back at Kreston, but his visage unnerved her. His eyes were fixed and his expression was as hard as the stone underfoot. He offered only a single nod, which she returned before she went her way, and he went his.

Each of the dozen panes in the Hall of Misted Mirrors tracked the souls that had filtered into the Realme. The only pane that did not was the prime pane, which displayed the conflict into which he had just dispatched Kreston and his Shadow Warriors.

The King of Shadows regarded it, and the battle's many participants, with derisive enjoyment, even as he collected the souls into pits below the other panes. Those souls, the remnants of mortals both cruel and kind, fell haplessly down, unable to escape as the king conjured more of the smokey tendrils that supported the panes. He transformed them into bars that sealed the pits. Then the king relished the plaintiff moans that rose up as he continued to watch the magenta landscape.

In her Twilight Grotto, the Raven Queen began to tremble with the strain of sealing the breach. A tear formed in her unblinking amethyst eye and rolled down her willow-white cheek. It dripped off of the side of her deep-red lips as she continued to focus on her task.

In the magenta landscape, Alerice cut cleanly through a lizard's tail, causing the beast to roar and writhe. She dodged the spray of its blood, but noticed Oddwyn backing from a lizard of his own. He was drawing too close to the acid.

"Oddwyn, look out!" she cried.

Oddwyn turned in her direction, but a sudden burst of blood pressure from the lizard's body sent a viscous blue spray over him. Blood covered his hair and face, and splotched his silver scale mail. He grimaced and wiped his mouth clean, flicking the lubricious blue off of his hand as he shook it.

Alerice reined up, bewildered.

"I thought you said it was acid."

"To you, mortal!" Oddwyn shouted in disgust. "Yeck!" he complained before he launched his iridescent chain about the dying lizard's neck. Alerice looked Oddwyn over, and then regarded the beast. She leaped toward it and hacked its head off in a scissor slice of her pixie poles.

In her Twilight Grotto, the Raven Queen gave up a mighty exhale, and the panes about her went dark.

In the magenta landscape, the atmosphere above stabilized, and the star clusters began to swirl along their previous currents.

Kreston skewered the final lizard, and stepped back to avoid its blood.

Alerice paced toward him, but his expression was still void of emotion. Even though the fight was over and everyone should be enjoying victory, Kreston Dühalde, the confidant who had shared her drink and the comrade who had stood at her side, was simply not there. He was obdurate, unable to recognize her with any warmth.

Oddwyn approached, the Raven Knights behind him. He watched as the Shadow Warriors appeared to flank Kreston, who leveled a steely gaze at the knights.

Alerice watched as Oddwyn took in the scene. He dismissed the Raven Knights and offered for Kreston to reciprocate. Kreston gestured with his broadsword for the Shadow Warriors to disperse. They obeyed, leaving Oddwyn and Kreston locking stares with one another.

Alerice looked between them, and then she looked farther away to see Ketabuck and the fauns leaving. She *clanged* her pixie poles to attract their attention, and as the clear tone rang out, she watched them pause and turn back. They bugled to her and raised their weapons in triumph. She raised a single pole to them in return.

Then she turned back to Kreston, unable to find joy in his presence. He was a man capable of wholesale slaughter, and it frightened her.

"Why did you help us?" she managed to ask.

"The king ordered it," Kreston said in an icy tone that Alerice had never heard before.

"But why?" she pressed.

"Ask the king," he said. He was about to wipe the blue blood from his blade in order to sheathe it, when he suddenly let out a sharp grunt as his left eye crimped shut.

Alerice looked at the King of Shadows' mark on Kreston's brow, but it was not glowing. Still, he reacted by gulping back the words, "I will!", so he was definitely reacting to some unheard voice.

Kreston grunted once more and then gave his head a single strong shake. He pressed his lips together and drew a breath through his nose, but then relaxed his stance.

"The king knows about the rips in the ether," he said. "And if *she* can't do something about it, he will."

"The Raven Queen has this in hand, *Captain*," Oddwyn said, emphasizing Kreston's rank in the same tenor he used to refer to the queen.

Kreston's grip tightened on his broadsword, but Alerice stepped between the two.

"Fighting each other solves nothing," she stated. "Oddwyn, you and I will go to her majesty and learn what she intends to do. Kreston, I do not know if you are my ally or my rival right now. You said yourself that you serve the king, so it has obviously suited him to have you here. You are good in a fight, no one can deny that. And for what it's worth, I personally thank you for helping us."

Kreston drew another breath and his shoulders relaxed a bit more. He finally looked at her with a hint of humanity, for which she was most grateful.

***

"My husband sent his champion," the Raven Queen commented. "The King of Shadows will not assist me openly, but he offered his help peripherally. That is interesting."

Alerice stood at the foot of the dais in the Hall of Eternity. The Raven Queen sat upon her throne, her Raven Knights behind her. Alerice studied her matron, searching for clues that might give up her mood, but she may as well have tried prying secrets out of a porcelain doll.

The Raven Queen sat with posture so straight that she seemed to be supported by an internal frame. She gazed forward, her amethyst eyes looking into some vast unknown. Her voice of dark honey was calm and measured, and the only hint that she may have suffered strain came from Oddwyn.

He stood beside Alerice, still dyed half-blue from the lizard's blood. Yet he focused intensely on the queen, and Alerice could see that regardless of his appearance, which in a more jovial setting would be quite comical, the mood was very serious.

"There is another rip applying pressure to the Evherealme," the queen said. The Queen's Eye rested in her lap. She glanced down upon it, and then returned to her faraway gaze. "I do not have the strength to open and seal it."

Alerice glanced at Oddwyn, who glanced back. Then she looked up at the queen.

"If it opens, will you be able to contain it?" she asked.

The Raven Queen swallowed delicately. The flash of her willow-white throat was her only movement.

"I do not know," she said softly.

Oddwyn seemed ready to begin pacing, but he held his place. Alerice, however, began to reflect on all that she had learned thus far. Her gaze shifted to the eyes of the Raven Knights, glowing golden spheres in the eye sockets of their full-metal helms. She studied the edges of their arm and leg plates that were crafted as metal feather tips, and looked at the feathered edges of their long black cloaks.

She recalled wearing one of those cloaks as she had destroyed Prince Vygar's sealed niches in the waterfall grotto. She had smashed each of the glyphs with a pixie pole before she had marched out with the faun spirits in tow. The souls had burst forth and flown away, and she wondered...

"My Queen? Could a rift in the Realme be opened into Mortalia?"

Both the queen and Oddwyn regarded her.

"How do you mean?" the Raven Queen asked.

"Well, aren't there places in the Realme that meld into Mortalia, the way Mortalia melds into the Realme through the Convergence?"

"There are," the queen replied.

"So, if you could direct the energy of this new breach to open into Mortalia, then whatever comes through would be set loose in the living world. I can fight it there. So can Oddwyn and the knights. I could possibly call upon the Wyld, and perhaps even the wizard Pauldin. But if you can expel energy into a world where the Realme will not bear the strain, you can seal the breach while I dispatch whatever invades."

Alerice paused a moment and then leaned in to Oddwyn to whisper, "You know that 'dispatch' means to kill, right?"

Oddwyn glared at Alerice from under his blue-covered brow, but she winked at him and his gaze softened.

The corner of the queen's deep-red lips turned up, and life seemed to rekindle in her amethyst eyes.

"You will need a colleague," she stated. "You have lived a secluded life in your tavern, Alerice, and though you may have heard of some wonders, you have yet to meet someone truly wondrous. Pauldin is not the man for this task. The person you require is the lady he lost, the sorceress Allya."

"Yes, My Queen," Alerice said. "How do I find her?"

"I will open a portal to her," the queen said. "I will tell her the reason for your arrival. She respects the Realme and its balance with Mortalia. She will lend herself to this fight, and perhaps become a source of inspiration for you. Like you, she has suffered personally for a life of greater meaning."

"It would be my pleasure to meet her," Alerice said with a reverence.

"It would be my pleasure to meet her," Oddwyn mimicked under his breath as he folded his arms and rolled his ice-blue eyes.

"Oddwyn?" the queen asked.

"Nothing, My Queen. I was just wondering how long it will take before Alerice needs my help."

"You don't think I can meet a sorceress?" Alerice asked.

"I think you still need help in a fight," Oddwyn replied. "You're getting better, but you're not ready to go into full battle yet, not on your own."

"She is not going to go on her own, Oddwyn," the queen stated. "She is going to go with Kreston."

Alerice opened her mouth to ask "What?", but all that came out was a throaty, "Erhh..."

"Ahmmm..." Oddwyn similarly declared.

Then they regarded one another before Alerice spoke.

"But, can I trust him?"

"A valid question," the queen said. "I have told you that he is the king's man. That said, I must consider the reason why the king sent him to aid you in sealing this latest breach. It was because my husband wished to gain some advantage.

"The King of Shadows will never act against me directly, nor I against him. He must have tasked Kreston with seeking what he desires. However, Kreston must work through you, Alerice, and if he fights at your side, you may be able to discover what the king wishes him to do."

Alerice glanced at Oddwyn, who grimaced awkwardly as if to say, "Are you sure about this?" Alerice set her shoulders.

"I will do as you say, My Queen."

"Alerice," the queen cautioned. "Remember that Kreston Dühalde is a man in great turmoil. What was done to him needed to be done."

Alerice considered the look she had just seen on Kreston's face – that of a man void of empathy whose only objective was to slay what lay before him. She shuddered at how cold his hazel eyes had become, and knew that perhaps the queen was right.

***

"Kreston, have you ever seen a fire opal?" Alerice asked.

"No," he replied. "Heard of them. Never seen one."

"I have. A wealthy man came to the Cup and Quill once, and he wore one centered in his amulet. They shimmer in colors of red and orange and blue-green."

"And?"

"And so I think this tower was crafted from giant slabs of them," she said as she beheld a magnificent stone structure that caught the daylight with a grace she could never have imagined.

Allya's tower looked to be hewn from polished opalescent blocks. It rose up two stories high and then spanned out into a pointed cap. The roofing tiles looked like wide, flat rubies, and the spike above appeared to be made of gold.

The tower stood on a rise in a rock basin, and a little lake had formed in the bowl. The surrounding stone presented colors of ruby, brown, and fuchsia. Festooning them were luscious draping vines bearing burgundy blooms. Fire spouts dotted the area, some flaming up in spurts, some burning constantly.

The energy of the place was that of a domesticated conflagration, alive and burning yet comfortable and hospitable. Alerice had no idea what source fueled the fire spouts or what water nourished the vines. She only knew that she could never have conjured such a place in her wildest dreams, and she was fairly certain that Kreston could not have either.

Alerice adjusted her studded belt and made certain that her weapons rested in their proper places. She felt for the Realme dagger at her hip, gripped it, and then gave it a pat. She took a confident breath, set her shoulders back, and prepared to step forward. After all, how often did one have the chance to make the acquaintance of a sorceress?

"Alerice," Kreston said.

She turned to him, but she had seen that guilt-ridden look before. He no doubt wanted to apologize for the way he had behaved when fighting the lizards, or more to the point, the way the King of Shadows had forced him to behave.

However, now was not the time. If he was being forced to plot against the Raven Queen, so be it. She needed his steel, and hopefully he could relax into simply being himself if she made that clear.

"Kreston, do you remember the evening we met?"

"Yes?"

"Do you remember that after you had heard your battlefield voices, you recovered yourself and then struck me across the jaw to prevent me from getting close to you?"

"Yes," he said, more regretfully.

"Well, I understand now that there are more than battlefield voices in your head. The king is there. Perhaps the queen as well. But we have work to do. Are you with me?"

Kreston stood straight and nodded.

Alerice softened her tone to add, "That's not to say I don't care about things that plague you. I do, and perhaps there is some way for us to sort it all out, but for the moment, we need to keep to our task."

Kreston offered her an "after you" gesture. Alerice smiled and turned toward the tower.

Alerice found herself looking about at a magnificent interior. Flaming golden sconces burned about the encircling walls. A curved staircase rose along the wall, ascending to the story above. Vaulting timbers joined at a central ring beam to support the roof, while vertical and horizontal beams jutted out from the curved ones to join the roof to the tower's walls. Fairy lights twinkled about the timbers in colors of pale red, white, and soft yellow.

Rich tapestries bearing images of Sukaar, Father God of Fire, hung on the wall before her, accenting the hall's most striking adornment – an altar standing in the tower's center, its rounded shape matching the hall. Its red stone bore wide black veins, and its golden top was dotted with cabochons of garnet and jet. The altar bore a hammered gilt basin in which burned an iridescent flame. Alerice stepped a bit closer to it and glanced inside. No fuel fed the blaze. It simply existed.

"So, where is she?" Kreston muttered from the side of his mouth.

Alerice did not know, for a portion of the tower's

exterior had simply faded open a moment ago to admit them.

"Here, Captain Dühalde," a woman said from behind.

Both Alerice and Kreston turned to see someone truly wondrous, as the Raven Queen had proffered.

Allya was a woman of Alerice's own height. She had rich auburn hair with pearl-and-golden highlights. Her eyes were emerald, but the most striking thing about her was that the left side of her torso bore a tremendous scar.

Indeed, her entire left breast had been burned away, leaving only blistered blotches and crinkled lines that were both hideous and beautiful. They glistened with the same fiery opalescence found in the tower's stone.

Alerice saw hints of ivory and gold in the grotesque skin, but what made Allya's disfigurement all the more intriguing was that the sorceress wore it openly. Her shimmering green gown was cut one-breasted so that it fell from the right side of her neck to her left hip. Indeed, while her right breast seemed perfectly intact, Allya's great scar was obviously a source of pride.

Alerice met Allya's emerald gaze and reverenced. "Sorceress."

"Ravensdaughter," Allya replied. She then regarded Kreston. "Captain."

"Madame," Kreston said with a formal bow.

The three passed an awkward moment, before

Alerice simply could not contain her childlike giddiness.

"This place is amazing," she exhaled.

Allya smiled. "I'm glad you enjoy it."

"Enjoy it?" Alerice said turning about as she held her hands out from her sides. "The whole tower is beyond belief. The stone basin outside is too. I mean, I've heard people spin tales of magical places. My Grammy Linden used to send me to sleep with them, but..."

Kreston stepped close to Alerice, grabbed the back of her studded belt, and gave it a yank.

Alerice collected herself as Allya came forward.

"Might I inquire about the burn?" Kreston asked.

"You may, Captain," Allya said.

"Actually," Alerice interjected. "He doesn't like being called Cap--"

Kreston yanked her belt once more, and stood his ground as Allya came before him.

She began running her fingertips about her scar, her hand moving over the many dimples and creases. The gesture was not meant to seduce, nor did Kreston appear to see it as such. Eventually, she passed her hand down to her hip and rested it at her side.

"This is unlike any wound you have ever seen, I would imagine," she said.

"It is, madame," he replied.

"That's because it was a gift. A loving gift from Sukaar himself. This..." She gestured to the area where her left breast had once been. "...is where he kissed me."

"Kissed you," Alerice said softly.

"Yes, Ravensdaughter. Just as the mark upon your brow is where the queen has kissed you." Allya glanced from Alerice's brow to Kreston's, but offered no comment on the mark left by the King of Shadows. "The gods above and below all claim us with signs we can never hide. Myself, I never wish to. I wear this scar openly so that all may see it and take heed."

"Of?" Kreston asked.

"Of this," Allya said gently as she raised her hands palms-up.

Fire shot up from her grasp. Alerice reflexively tried to step backward, but Kreston tightened his grip on her belt and forced her to stand her ground.

Allya, however, did step back to set her full body alight. Alerice could feel the heat. The sorceress smiled as flames licked about her face. Her green gown shimmered all the more brightly, reflecting the orange-gold of the dancing inferno, and just as with Belmaine, Alerice wondered if the sorceress was about to weaponize her scintillation.

"You needn't worry," Allya said in a voice that half-echoed about the tower. She drew the fire back into her palms, and with a graceful wave of both hands, she caused the flames to reduce down to red wisps that floated about her fingertips. "The Raven Queen has explained the reason for your visit."

Kreston released Alerice's belt and bowed once again. Alerice, however, was transfixed on the sorceress' scar, which now danced with light like embers glowing in a pit.

***

"By design, our world and the Evherealme are not meant to meld into one another, save for at a few specific points," Allya said as she led Alerice and Kreston from her tower's entrance, down the short rise, and toward the stone basin's little lake.

Alerice fought the distraction of the flame spouts above and around, doing her best to listen.

"The Raven Queen sent you to me as the best hope to induce a meld, though what we truly require is a devotee of Imari, Mother Goddess of Water and Wind. Such a devotee would be able to calm things better than I. However, I have not known the Great Mother to bless anyone in my lifetime, and so we must work with Father Fire's power to tear open a rift."

"But isn't a rift the sort of thing the Raven Queen has been trying to prevent?" Alerice asked.

"It is," Allya answered. "Yet, it is the only way for the queen to direct the energy of an abscess into our world. I will manage the breach here with your assistance, and she will lance it, forcing the energy to us."

"What assistance?" Kreston asked.

Allya paused to regard them both. "You two are

Realme Walkers, but you cannot create your own portals. However, I need a gateway to the Realme in order to control whatever the queen sends us. She will not be able to create a portal because she will be overseeing the abscess, but you can create a joint one by using the king's Shadow Warriors and the queen's Raven Knights."

Alerice was not certain this was a good idea, for she had brought Kreston to fight, not solicit the King of Shadows.

"What about Oddwyn?" she asked.

Allya smiled. "Oddwyn is a dear soul, but I need more than he, or she, can offer. I need the two of you. While I concentrate the power of the Great Father, you will call for the warriors and the knights. You can use their essences, which in truth is their majesties' essences, to affect a gateway."

Alerice noted Kreston's tension.

"Is there any way I can open a gateway myself?" she asked.

"Just set it in motion," Kreston said flatly.

Alerice wanted to say something that might spare him the indignity of calling upon the king only to be denied, but she could see that he was ready to act, do or die.

"We need to take up positions about the lake," Allya said. "A triangle will give us the best advantage. I will move to the stone overhang just there. Alerice, stay where you are, and, Captain--"

"I see it," Kreston said, noting a flat boulder that

completed the required formation.

"Very well, let's begin," Allya said.

Alerice watched Allya and Kreston move toward their places. Having no idea which weapons would suit the moment, she drew the pixie pole cylinders from her belt and focused her spirit on the mark of the Raven Queen.

She allowed her soul to 'open' through it as though she were opening her own personal portal to the Realme. She felt it pulse upon her brow even as she concentrated on the air before her. She willed the world about her to swirl with the signature tri-colors of black, midnight blue, and deep teal.

As she did, she wondered if she would be able to create her own portals someday. If she was destined to be a Realme Walker, she couldn't rely on portals crafted by others. Independence was key to agility, and if the Raven Queen needed her to perform at her best, she required autonomy.

"My Queen," Alerice called mentally into the ether.

Standing within the magenta landscape, Oddwyn at her side and her Raven Knights behind, the Raven Queen raised her willow-white face to the swirling star clusters. Her Eye floated above her left palm, and she smiled, for Alerice's voice did not simply ring in her mind. It echoed across the atmosphere with a clarity previously unknown.

Oddwyn looked up. Then he regarded his mistress. "That was strong."

"It was," the queen said as she held both palms before her so that the Queen's Eye rested above them. Focusing her amethyst gaze upon the gem, she caused its glow to intensify and its inner essence to churn.

"*I am prepared, Alerice,*" she mentally conveyed.

In the stone basin, Alerice felt the queen's words sounding through her. She saw the magenta landscape in her mind's eye, and she nearly reeled at the synergy of spirit she shared with the world below. She felt as though she herself was the gateway between Mortalia and the Evherealme. It was as though she stood at once between the two places, and wondered what might happen if she called upon the qualities of either world to meld through her.

"Alerice!" she heard Kreston call.

Alerice startled back to the present and regarded him. He stood upon his boulder, broadsword in hand.

"Get your poles ready!" he ordered.

It was an order, not that Alerice objected. In point of fact, she was glad to have a bit of direction to steel herself from the throes of the inter-worldly connection she somehow knew she had just created.

She activated her pixie poles so that the blades popped out, and stood on her guard. She then looked between Kreston and Allya, noticing that they regarded her in a strange manner, almost as though they were both awestruck. Precisely why, she had no idea, but it was best not to wonder, for it was time to get to work.

She raised one pole in salute to Kreston, who raised his broadsword in reply before he looked at Allya and gestured his blade in her direction.

Allya nodded to Kreston and to Alerice. Then she held out a palm toward them both.

All the fire spouts about the basin suddenly flared up as Allya called to Sukaar, Father God of Fire. She sent out flaming beams toward Alerice and Kreston, refining them until they became luminescent red-orange rays. She aimed her power at the marks upon their brows, and as they struck, stunning both Realme Walkers, she instructed, "Reach out to one another."

Alerice leveled a pixie pole at Kreston, who leveled his broadsword at her. Red-orange rays shot out from the tips of both weapons to complete the triangle.

"Tell the queen we are ready, Alerice," Allya commanded.

"Yes," Alerice said before she mentally called, *"Send the Raven Knights, My Queen."*

Alerice's words echoed across the magenta sky, affecting the starry swirls. The Raven Queen focused upon her Eye even as she drew down a bulge from the 'sky' above. It grew bulbous with multiple blotchy pockets that threatened to spew forth whatever contents they contained.

Oddwyn drew and activated his own set of pixie poles as he stood protectively at the queen's side. The

Raven Knights each held up their two-handed blades.

Atop his boulder, Kreston tried to center himself enough to reach out to the King of Shadows. However, the energy swell filling him struck his senses. All he could see when he looked at Allya was a woman of such living dynamic that he felt alive in her fire. She was as intoxicating as Belmaine, Goddess of Passion and Chaos, only he did not desire her. He did, however, feel the power of a dozen horses in his heart as her strength filled him.

Then he gazed upon Alerice. How could she have known that she had just caused the air about her to dance as though she were a living portal? How could she have known that the mark upon her brow had glowed so brightly that he had nearly cowered before it as he might before *her*? And yet he had felt no fear or touch of madness. Clearly, Alerice possessed talents that she had yet to discover.

Kreston forced the myriad of sensations to the back of his brain. He concentrated on the accursed mark scratched upon his brow, and conjured the image of the king's prime pane hanging in his Hall of Misted Mirrors.

"Give me your Shadows, My King!"

The King of Shadows reacted to Kreston's voice emanating from his crystal-crowned mirror. He paused from the enjoyment of sending shock bursts into one of his captured souls and turned to the pane. He conjured the sight of Kreston standing atop a boulder in the stone basin, and upon adjusting the view to see through Kreston's eyes, he beheld the girl and the sorceress.

"To help them? I think not."

Kreston drew up his courage amid the rush of vitality to risk the tone that he reserved only when correcting a superior officer at a dire moment.

"You want the Eye? Give me your damned Shadows!"

The king reacted with incredulity. It would be a simple matter to draw Kreston back to the Realme for a reprimand, but as he paused to consider the moment, he activated another pane.

The Raven Queen stood in the open magenta landscape. She bore her Eye, which the king found deliciously enticing.

"They're yours," he said to Kreston.

In the landscape, the Raven Queen bade her Raven Knights to take flight toward the globular distortion overhead. They spread their feathered, black cloaks into wings and launched themselves upward, flying at the abscess from opposite directions. Then they extended their two-handed blades and carved slices as they flew toward one another.

The queen caused her Eye to glow exponentially. An atmospheric pustule burst above her, and she directed her Raven Knights to circle about the incoming deluge. They began spiraling so quickly that they created a meniscus that held the abscess' discharge in place.

The Raven Queen directed them to come abreast of one another and fly up into the breach's center. They did, drawing the abscess into the vacuum of their wake. The Raven Queen then used her force of will to thrust the Evherealme's power after them, shoving the ulcerous energy into Mortalia.

In his Hall of Misted Mirrors, the King of Shadows watched his wife. He gestured for his Shadow Warriors to come forth, which they did, blending in with the surrounding smoke tendrils that bore the mirrors. With a quick wave, he banished them to Kreston's side.

"Here it is!" Allya shouted.

The little lake bubbled, then roiled, then erupted in a great upward splash that inundated Alerice and Kreston. Yet, focused on their course, they did not react as the Raven Knights emerged from the lake, followed by the Shadow Warriors.

Alerice and Kreston held wide their arms so that their respective guardians could flank them. The knights and warriors alighted abreast of them, and Alerice and Kreston tapped their strength while raising their hands to the lake.

As though their mental visions had joined, they both saw that a tremendous gash had opened along the lake's bottom. Together they used the Realme's power to seal it.

Allya collected the power of the roaring fire

spouts to break the triangular beams she had created, and redirect the energy into the lake. She caused a bed of multi-colored coral to weave about the gash and stitch it closed so that Alerice and Kreston could step away.

Both Alerice and Kreston felt the break in Allya's contact and nearly fell to their knees. Kreston quickly regained his balance atop his boulder while Alerice stumbled a few paces before she found her footing. They both shook their senses clear, and then regarded each other as though they had successfully crossed the finish line of a race.

In the magenta landscape, the queen sealed the breach above. Oddwyn breathed a sigh of relief as the queen allowed her Eye to float freely.

"Knights, return to me," she said.

In his Hall of Misted Mirrors, the King of Shadows smiled as he called to his crystal-crowned pane, "Shadows."

The king then glanced at the exhausted soul beside him. With a final volley of shocks, he caused it to gyrate, scream, and rupture.

In the stone basin, Alerice watched the Raven Knights spread their cloaks and take flight. In the blink of an eye, they were out of sight. She looked at Kreston, only to watch the Shadow Warriors dissolve in dark gray wisps.

Then she regarded the lake, which had begun

forming multiple bubbling domes.

"Kreston...?" she asked.

Kreston looked at the water.

"This isn't over," he called as he leaped down from the boulder and hurried for Alerice.

"Move to higher ground," Allya called out in a voice that, while physical, also resonated mentally. Alerice and Kreston could see the marks glowing on one another's brows, and as they met on the sandy lakeshore, they turned together and hurried toward the rise that led up to the sorceress' tower.

The lake's domes were on the verge of bursting. Allya summoned more power from the flare spouts and cast a ring of flame that evaporated several domes into fumaroles.

The domes centered within the lake exploded. Otherworldly neighs sounded as silvery, green-blue horses leaped forth from each. Their eyes burned red. Their front teeth were long and sharp. Their manes and tails were made of twined river grass, and their powerful bodies heaved as they blew foaming water from their nostrils.

"Kelpies!" Kreston shouted as he helped Alerice up the rise.

"What?" she asked, taking a stand with her pixie poles ready.

Kreston glanced over his shoulder as he protectively placed himself before her. "Kelpies. Water demons. Don't let them get near you. If you touch them, you'll stick to them and they'll drag you into the lake and drown you."

"Gods above!" Alerice exclaimed.

Four kelpies neighed, their terrible voices echoing about the stone basin. They fixed their stares on Kreston and Alerice and charged, galloping atop the lake's surface and churning up foam in their wake.

"What do we do?" Alerice half-shouted.

Kreston glanced at her weapons. "Get your bow. You need range when dealing with these things!"

Kreston threw his broadsword at the nearest kelpie. It impaled the monster, which gave up a bloodcurdling neigh as the sword passed through its body. The kelpie reared, but then it congealed into a viscous blue-gray ooze that gushed onto the water's surface and dissolved.

Kreston held his hand high, and his broadsword reappeared in his grip. He threw it at the next kelpie, likewise congealing it into blue-gray ooze.

Alerice retracted her pixie poles and drew her Realme crossbow. She glanced up at Allya, who was directing her fire to move in from the lake's perimeter in order to close on more bubble domes.

Alerice aimed at one of the two incoming kelpies. Her crossbow's string pulled back of its own accord, and a gleaming black bolt appeared in the flight groove. She pulled the trigger into the tiller and the bolt struck home.

The kelpie reeled with a wild whinny. As the dark glow of the bolt's impact spread over its torso, the beast dissolved into its own clot of blue-gray ooze and sank below the water's surface.

Kreston advanced to throw his blade at another kelpie, which was nearly upon him, and Alerice watched in horror as he closed the distance.

"Kreston!" she called as she leveled her bow for another shot.

Kreston came before the monster, which reared and kicked its forehooves. He dodged and thrust his broadsword into the creature's chest. It reeled, but still bit at him, tearing the shoulder of his worn uniform. A crossbow bolt struck its red eye, and it reeled again before rupturing into a blue-gray oozy mass that soaked Kreston's head and shoulders.

He withdrew his blade and wiped his face clear as he turned toward the lake to size up any other targets.

In his Hall of Misted Mirrors, the King of Shadows moved before his crystal-crowned pane. He saw the Raven Queen standing with Oddwyn. Her Eye floated above her willow-white palms. The king smiled and traced the nail of his index finger vertically down the pane.

Standing atop the magenta landscape's light gray stone, Oddwyn and the Raven Queen surveyed the sealed breach. The work would hold.

Oddwyn looked aside to find the two Raven Knights flying in. However, he noticed a little crevasse open in midair near the edge of the starry clusters.

"My Queen?" he said, regarding her to make certain he had her attention, then pointing at the crevasse.

The crevasse tore downward and split in half. Bright green light shone out as it began to pull apart.

The queen's amethyst eyes widened, and she turned fully to the rift, directing her Eye to float before her so that she might draw upon its power.

"Knights!" Oddwyn ordered.

Alerice paced a step down the rise as she leveled her crossbow at another forming kelpie, shooting it before it could fully emerge from its bubble dome. She paced another step and then another as she continued to fire, grateful that her bow reloaded in rapid succession.

She saw Allya begin to blast kelpies with fireballs even as her still-flaming ring scintillated kelpies at the water's edge. Each disappeared in steam plumes that mirrored the basin's flame spouts.

Alerice watched Kreston throw his blade to slay another kelpie, and as its neigh rang out, she looked for another target. Just then a bubble dome appeared before her and a kelpie burst forth, showering her with lake foam.

Alerice tucked her head, and then wiped the water from her eyes and looked up. The kelpie sprang forth and vaulted over her, easily clearing her as Jerome had cleared the Wyld warriors when battling Belmaine. It landed behind her, turned about, and reared.

"Alerice!" Kreston shouted.

Alerice tried to aim her bow, but the kelpie lashed out with its forehooves and kicked her hard in the chest. She flew to the sandy lakeshore, her wind knocked out, and was unable to protect herself from the vicious teeth baring down.

She caught sight of the kelpie's blazing red eyes as it snatched hold of her and tossed her up onto its back. Then it reared high and neighed wildly before it landed on all fours and bolted for the water.

"Alerice!" she heard both Kreston and Allya cry as she tried to leap down. However, her legs stuck to the kelpie's ribs and her hands stuck to its shoulders. She tugged and struggled, but in moments it had splashed into the lake and dove down.

Alerice barely had time to draw a deep breath as her head went under. She continued to struggle, all the while hearing the kelpie's neigh bubbling about her ears as might a ghost's haunting howls.

She tugged and tugged, but soon she felt dizzy. It became difficult to move, and she began to feel as though she were floating. She looked up at the water's surface, seeing twinkles of sunlight, and possibly hints of Allya's encircling flames, and while she knew she was in the utmost danger, she could not help but become transfixed by the softly enchanting spectacle.

Until a crossbow bolt *whizzed* in and a dark flash burst before her. She felt the kelpie rear under her, and then she felt nothing below her legs. She tried to kick in hopes that she might have the strength to move, but her body began to go limp.

Alerice felt someone grab her arm and yank her upward, dragging her toward the surface as though she were a lump of wet laundry. Before she knew it, her head splashed out from the lake, and she tried to breathe. Then she quickly fell into a violent coughing fit as her lungs did their best to expel the water she had inhaled.

Someone wrapped a strong arm about her and pulled her close. He swam with her to the water's edge, even as the encircling line of flames parted to permit them access to the shore.

Still coughing and unable to gain her bearings, Alerice felt someone sit behind her, his chest pressed against her back to prop her up. Then she saw a man's hands forcing her crossbow into hers.

"Fire it, Alerice," Kreston said over her shoulder. "You're the only one who can load it. Thank the gods you had one bolt ready when the kelpie took you, but you've got to keep shooting."

Still coughing, Alerice managed to comprehend what needed to be done. She leveled her crossbow at the few remaining kelpies. Allya's fire blasts landed on others while she shot, noting how Kreston helped her aim and pull the trigger into the tiller.

As the next few moments flashed past her eyes, Alerice finally saw her black bolt strike the last kelpie, which dissolved into blue-gray ooze that floated like dark scum on the water's foam.

Then the foam sank and the lake became calm. The encircling fire died, and Alerice looked up to see Allya standing tall on her stone outcrop, the scar across the left side of her body glowing brightly.

Alerice felt Kreston pull her close and hold her. She coughed one last time, and relaxed into him. He brought his cheek against her head, and she responded by nuzzling against it. Then she felt him tremble slightly, which caused her to move away.

"Kreston?" she asked softly over her shoulder.

Kreston released her and stood. She looked up at him, seeing his expression of anger and desperation, but also relief. He extended his hand, which she took so that he could help her up to her feet. She wobbled a bit, and he reached out to steady her.

Her crossbow rested on the shore. She bent down to take hold of it and looked it over. Then she noticed Kreston looking her over. Apparently satisfied that she was restored, he held his hand high and his broadsword appeared in his palm. He sheathed it, and Alerice turned to locate Allya.

Then she heard Oddwyn calling, "Alerice! Get down here!"

"Did you hear that?" she asked Kreston.

"Yes," he said, looking about. He pointed to the signature tri-color black, midnight blue, and deep teal of a nascent Realme portal. "There."

"Go!" Allya called in a voice that was again both physical and mental.

Alerice leveled her bow and charged for the portal, Kreston running behind her.

***

In the Evherealme's magenta landscape, seven wyverns circled above the Raven Queen and Oddwyn, churning the starry clusters into wild patterns in the wake of their flight.

Each Raven Knight had engaged a wyvern, slashing with their two-handed blades as the creatures fought back with claws and teeth. The remaining five targeted the Raven Queen.

Using her Eye, she attempted to seal the breach feeding strength to the beasts. Oddwyn glanced over his shoulder at the open Realme portal, but quickly shifted his attention back to a wyvern that had begun a strafing run.

He summoned his iridescent chain and began twirling it. The wyvern drew close and opened its jaws. Oddwyn leaped high and cast the chain, which coiled about the wyvern's mouth and lashed its jaws shut.

It immediately banked hard and beat its wings to gain altitude, drawing up Oddwyn and snapping the chain from his hold, which cast him across the landscape. Able to glide within the Realme, Oddwyn banked hard and shot back for the Raven Queen, sweeping her aside as the wyvern scraped the chain off its jaws with its hind claws.

Oddwyn looked up at the beast's yellow-green

eyes, only to see one struck by a black crossbow bolt. The impact's dark glow radiated about the wyvern's head, and it breathed out a misaimed green fire burst as it reeled and careened, dead on the stone.

Oddwyn looked in the direction of the open portal, much relieved to see Alerice standing before it, crossbow aimed for another shot.

"Alerice!" he called, summoning a bladed pixie pole into his hand and raising it in salute.

Alerice raised her hand back at Oddwyn, but as he took up another protective stance before the queen, she glanced over her shoulder and said to an approaching Kreston, "The queen is here. Stay back."

She saw Kreston stop in his tracks and look past her. Then he averted his gaze.

"I'll take care of this," Alerice said as she charged into the fray.

Kreston watched her go, never feeling more impotent in his life. How could Alerice jump into this fight when he stood by and did nothing?

His blood began to boil as he glanced askance at the Raven Queen. He stepped out from the portal, daring to behold what he could of her. As long as he did not look at her damned purple eyes, he could manage this.

Here, now, in the chaos, when the heat of battle caused the most confusion, he had a chance to do his master's bidding, though he hated to. He hated the king for enslaving him. He hated himself for having become enslaved, but he could not stand against the King of Shadows.

But get *her* Eye, and perhaps the king might finally release him. That's why the king had called to him in the previous battle, causing his eye to crimp. "Gain her trust," the king had said, and this he had done, though for reasons that were solely his own.

But now he could use that trust. Implicate Alerice, and the queen might release her. It was his only option, and so he began to stalk Alerice as she shot down another wyvern.

Above, the Raven Knights each slew their beasts and flew to attack others. The final two wyverns circled, looking down at their marks.

Oddwyn saw one targeting him, and he moved away from the Raven Queen to lure it off of her position.

Alerice saw the other gazing down upon her with its steady yellow-green gaze. She raised her crossbow, smiling as she aimed. The bow's string pulled back, a gleaming black bolt appeared in the flight groove, and she fired. The bolt sailed with ease, striking it down.

Alerice leveled her bow upon the final beast. The crossbow self-loaded again and she took aim, but Kreston appeared beside her and snatched the bow from her grasp.

"Kreston," she said, turning about to behold him. "What are you doing?"

Kreston looked down upon Alerice, ice in his veins, and grabbed her tightly. He pulled her close and pressed his brow to hers so that the marks glowing upon their foreheads touched.

"Do as I say!" he ordered in her mind, stunning her. *"Admit this was your choice!"*

Alerice trembled helplessly as Kreston placed the bow back in her hands, helped her level it at Oddwyn, and fired. The bolt struck Oddwyn in the shoulder, and he cried out as he fell. Kreston averted the queen's deadly amethyst gaze as she turned toward him, and then threw his broadsword at her with all his might.

He heard her scream. He heard Oddwyn call to her, and then he heard the glassy tinkle of the Queen's Eye falling to the pooled light gray stone.

Kreston bolted for the gem, diving for it and clutching it as he rolled forward into a stance. He turned about and hurled it into the still-open portal. Then he felt, more than heard, a hand catch it.

The King of Shadows appeared within the portal's opening, the Eye in his grasp. He held his free hand forward, and the broadsword he had bequeathed to Kreston appeared in his grip. He gestured it toward his side, and Kreston disappeared from his stance and reappeared to flank him.

The king held up the Eye to examine its inner gray swirl, and then shifted his gaze up at the remaining wyvern. With a surge of his own psychic force, he directed the Eye's energy at the beast. He called down the atmosphere's starry clusters to envelope it. Each luminous glow responded, leaching into the monster's scales and dissolving it midair so that its outline took on the stars' semblance before it joined their swirling cluster.

Oddwyn pulled the bolt from his shoulder, looked at it, and regarded Alerice. Then he looked at the felled queen, and cast the bolt aside as he dove for her, lifting her unconscious body into his arms.

"My Queen," he called as he moved her black hair from her willow-white face. He stroked her cheek, and she nestled against his hand. Oddwyn then presented her maiden self, and as the Raven Queen slowly regained consciousness, Oddwyn looked at Alerice, betrayal in her ice-blue eyes.

"Why?"

Alerice stared numbly at her crossbow. Unable to fathom all that had just transpired, she only knew one response, which she offered in a voice that did not seem to be hers.

"It was my choice."

Alerice watched Oddwyn regard her with a mixture of hurt and disbelief. She looked at the Raven Queen's body slumped in Oddwyn's embrace. Then she looked down at her bow – and suddenly she recalled everything.

Her head snapped up, and she glared at Kreston.

"What did you do?" she demanded.

The King of Shadows stepped forward to loom large. Even though he did not stand close, Alerice still backed a step.

"Go back to the witch," the king said, opening a portal and using the Queen's Eye to shove Alerice through it.

***

Alerice woke in a soft bed, wrapped in the comfort of a plush blanket. She wore only her black shirt and leggings. Glancing aside, she saw her scale mail tunic draped next to her, along with her studded belt.

She gazed overhead to find the interior of a roof's pointed cap. Support beams crossed above, dotted with fairy lights that twinkled in pale red, white, and soft yellow. A magnificent chandelier hung from the central crossbeams, but it bore no candles. Rather, iridescent flares sprang up from each dish to bathe the room in a warm glow.

Alerice smiled and turned to her other side to find Allya seated next to her in a carved armchair decorated with embroidered red upholstery.

"How long have I been here?" she asked.

"A few hours," Allya replied. "It's after nightfall. And you're welcome to stay the night. In truth, I wouldn't mind if you stayed a few days. You're quite a woman, Alerice Linden."

"Mmmm," Alerice commented. "Did the Raven Queen tell you my full name?"

"She did."

"Ah... oh!" Alerice said, sitting up. "The queen. Oddwyn. Allya, there was a fight in the Realme. And... And Kreston! Allya, he used me to attack them."

"Did he," Allya commented. "I didn't think he was that desperate."

Alerice looked at the sorceress. Then she pulled the blanket off and moved over to sit at the bedside.

"What do you mean desperate?" Alerice asked. "Kreston just betrayed me. How could he do that?"

"My dear, the King of Shadows tasked Kreston with capturing the Queen's Eye. I heard him say this when calling for the Shadow Warriors. He cannot disobey the king any more than you can disobey the queen."

Alerice considered her words and realized this was true. Both Kreston and the queen had warned her. Now it had happened, even though she did not wish to believe it.

"He was right to tell me that I could never trust him. I'll never make that mistake again."

"Alerice," Allya said gently. "I don't know if this will help, but for what it's worth, I can tell you that Kreston did not act according to his own desire."

"How do you know?"

"Because Kreston Dühalde is in love with you."

"With me?"

"Oh, yes. Quite deeply, I would say."

"Allya, anyone who loves someone would never betray them."

"Unless he believed he was doing the right thing."

Alerice looked Allya over. "What do you mean?"

"You should have seen Kreston's near-panic when the kelpie took hold of you," she said. "He threw his sword at it, but it dove underwater and he missed. He saw that you had dropped your bow on the shoreline, and he snatched it up as he dove in after you.

"Then when he brought you to the surface and swam with you to the shore, it was all he could do to keep himself from pressing you close. He focused his feelings into action, because that's what military men do. He helped you fight off the last kelpie, and then he shoved his feelings down as far as he could so as not to cling to you.

"You see, Alerice, I know the type of man whom the King of Shadows takes into his service. Kreston is one of those men, and now he may see you as his only hope to live, which is likely why he did what he did."

"Yes, he does see me that way," Alerice said before she drew and released a breath. "What... What sort of man does the king take?"

"All men of fighting stature have heard of the King of Shadows," Allya offered. "He is thought to have the power to defeat a man's enemies, and he bestows this power upon those who prove themselves worthy.

"So what type of man desires the king's power?" Allya continued. "There are two types. The first is a man of ego and ambition. This man craves power for power's sake and will do anything to achieve it. He will endure the physical rigors required in order to gain the king's attention, and will revel in the righteousness of wielding the king's blade."

"And the other?" Alerice asked.

"The other is the broken man who still has the strength to seek revenge. He is a lost soul, likely due to his own bad judgment or sometimes the victim of one bad decision. This is a man who, at heart, wants to right the wrongs he has created. He isn't seeking power for his own sake, but to correct some egregious error. I would place Kreston in this category."

Alerice nodded. "So does the Raven Queen. She told me once that Kreston is a broken man, wounded and confused. I've heard him call to a man named Landrew. I think that was his lieutenant. I think Kreston ordered him to attack a hill.

"Oh, and now that I think about it, when Kreston and I were in Basque, the Reef there noted his uniform and asked if he had been part of the Crimson Brigade. I said that I had heard about the brigade's ghost... Allya, you don't think that's Kreston, do you?"

Allya's silence spoke volumes. Alerice pressed her hand to her mouth and said softly into her fingers, "Gods above."

"As I said, the latter," Allya commented. "I believe he seeks to be free, but he's trapped."

"He is. And he wants to escape more than anything."

"Then Kreston may have betrayed you in order to

accomplish that goal. But you are still in service to the Raven Queen. You still bear her armor and her weapons, so Kreston's attempt has likely failed."

Alerice began drumming her fingers on her thigh.

"I've got to do something."

Allya smiled. "I admire your courage, Alerice. And your fortitude. I can see why the Raven Queen wished to take you into her service. Do you know why she has not had a champion for so long a time?"

"Why?" Alerice asked, cocking her head slightly to the side.

"Firstly, because Realme Walkers are not born all that often, but mostly because no one seeks the queen looking for power or prestige. She prefers to take someone's measure. That is perhaps the difference between them. The king is impetuous, whereas she is methodical."

"I wish I could knock their heads together and make them both see reason," Alerice said. "I used to do it all the time at the Cup and Quill. I negotiated more arguments than I can recall."

"Yes, I can see that in you."

"But the king and queen are acting like a rival brother and sister, and the only thing children respond to is a strong parent, especially a father."

"I can't imagine what type of father could dominate the King of Shadows and the Raven Queen, Alerice."

"Nor can I..." Alerice said, but her voice trailed off as she began to study the blotches and crinkles of

Allya's scarred body.

Allya regarded her line of sight, and then her own body, and she looked up sharply.

"You're not thinking of Sukaar?"

"He's the Father God of Fire."

"Alerice, listen to me," Allya said, leaning in. "You must be an accomplished person of magic for Sukaar to grant you his power, and while you are a natural Walker, you are nowhere near the level he seeks in a devotee."

"But, could it be enough for him to lend me the power to make the king and queen listen?"

"Sukaar does not lend anything. He gives his power to those who are willing to sacrifice to attain it."

Alerice settled herself and said, "Allya, I understand, but I need to be honest with you. This is not about Kreston. This is not about my service to an immortal who is at war with her husband. This is about the Realme.

"The king and queen behave the way they do because they face no consequences. Perhaps if they did, they might reconsider their motives. Does Sukaar have the power to make them listen? Is he wise enough to set them on a better course? The Realme will become more unbalanced as the king and queen argue. In the end, I don't believe that's what either of them want."

Allya sat back and considered everything for a moment. She looked about her bedchamber and gestured for the flames burning in the chandelier to rise up slightly. Eventually, she regarded Alerice, who had not broken eye contact.

"He does have the power," she said. "And he is wise enough, but Alerice, what are you willing to give up in order to have Sukaar do what you ask?"

"Whatever he takes," Alerice said.

***

Alerice stood with Allya in her tower's lower hall. Now that night had fallen, the fire burning atop the altar appeared far more brilliant. Alerice could not deny that she feared what she was about to attempt. However, she had set her mind to this task, come what may, and she trusted that Allya would do her best to intervene if the Father God of Fire became angry enough to wish her dead.

For some reason, she heard the King of Shadows' voice in her head reciting the admonition he had given when they had met.

"Wear your fear openly," he had said. "Show it for all to see. Only by exposing it shall you master it."

Very well. If she trembled a bit, let Sukaar see. Perhaps it was a good sign to show her apprehension and still stand tall. If she could do so in the Evherealme, she could do so now.

"Are you prepared?" Allya asked. "Because once I summon him, there will be a price to pay, no matter what happens, and he will know that you are the one who has requested his presence."

Alerice took a shallow breath, held it for a moment as she closed her eyes, and then exhaled as she set her shoulders and regarded the sorceress.

"I'm prepared."

"Very well."

Allya turned and paced to her altar. The iridescent flame lapped as it burned in the hammered gilt basin. Allya placed her hands into it and held them there as she aligned her spirit with Sukaar's essence. Then she began to chant.

> "Sukaar, Father Fire, listen to my voice.
> Sukaar, Father Fire, you are my love and choice.
> Sukaar, Father Fire, come to my domain.
> Sukaar, Father Fire, your power I maintain."

Allya repeated the chant, and as she did the flames grew taller. The iridescence gave off an otherworldly light, and Alerice could feel power building inside it. The flames burning in the sconces began to dim as though the altar was drawing in the air which gave them life, and as Alerice focused on Allya, she watched her skin glow in tones of living pearl, much as had Belmaine's. The sorceress' scar came alive with hints of light, again like embers glowing in a pit.

Suddenly, the flames died in the bowl, and as Allya continued to chant, Alerice saw something undulate in their place. She could not be certain at first, for the small mass that coiled and heaved appeared to be liquid gold. Yet as it grew more solid, Alerice saw the unmistakable shape of golden serpent scales.

The coils writhed, growing in girth until they filled the bowl to its rim. Ever expanding, the coils crested the bowl and began cascading over its sides. Alerice saw no head or tail, no fangs or rattles. Only the coils, which, as they grew still larger, took on a fiery quality as though an artist had brushed the golden serpent with tones of pink, pale orange, and ruby.

Then the coils expanded from the bowl, spilled out across the altar, and slumped onto the floor. They grew to the size of tree trunks, and Alerice found herself taking a step back as Allya finished her chanting and stood still.

"Stay where you are," Allya warned. "Let him examine you."

Alerice muscled her way through a nervous gulp and did as Allya instructed.

The coils expanded to her feet and began rubbing against her legs. Their sheer strength threatened to knock Alerice from her stance, but she employed a balance trick that she had learned when carrying heavy trays ladened with tankards – move one foot slightly behind the other and bend the knees. It had worked quite well at the Cup and Quill, and it worked quite well now.

"Allya, my love," a man's voice called from somewhere behind the altar. The coils continued to expand until they were so large that they filled the hall's inner circumference.

"My passionate father," Allya said.

She fell into a deep curtsey so that her front knee touched the floor, and she held the position. She gently reached back toward Alerice and offered a little hand flick to indicate that she should also assume a deferential posture. Alerice offered her customary reverence, but judging the move insufficient, she lowered herself to one knee while arching her back and setting her shoulders.

The serpent's head finally rose from the coils at the altar's opposite side, and Alerice found herself looking at a spectacle so dazzling that she nearly felt the need to shelter her gaze.

The supernatural viper bore a diamond head and piercing eyes alive with flame. Its coils gave off light, and as with the stone composing Allya's tower, each scale seemed to be created from a fire opal.

Alerice's fear melted into sheer awe. She felt excited, even giddy. She found it nearly impossible to contain the same childlike fascination that she had felt for Allya's home, and she was glad that Kreston was not here to yank the back of her belt to silence her.

"Great God!" she exclaimed. "Father Fire!"

"Alerice," Allya cautioned. "I have not yet presented you."

"Allya, my beloved," Sukaar said as his head rose toward the ceiling timbers. The fairy lights intensified near him. "I am not offended. Introduce us."

Allya stood and offered a head bow. Then she

gestured for Alerice to rise and stand abreast of her. Alerice did, unable to feel her own feet as she moved. Indeed, this was all too marvelous.

"Sukaar, Great Father Fire," Allya said. "May I present Alerice Linden of Navre, the Raven Queen's Realme Walker."

Alerice reverenced, for she now felt it appropriate, and waited for Allya to encourage the next move.

Sukaar tilted his head so that he could better examine Alerice. The flame within his eyes burned brightly, and in the next moment Sukaar transformed into a man.

His clothes were ruby velvet and gold, trimmed with black opal and garnet. His long hair was flaming red, though he had drawn his bangs into a woven knot at the back of his head. His eyes danced with the same fire as in his serpentine form, but then changed to a rich black dashed with gold.

He stepped forward toward Allya and reached a palm to her cheek. Heat radiated from his touch. Sukaar brushed his fingertips along her scar's pooled and cracked skin, red wisps floating from his nails as he lightly scratched her.

Alerice could see that Allya found the contact erotic, and watched as the sorceress reacted as any lover would when caught in the spell of her master's will.

Sukaar centered his fingers over the area where Allya's left breast had been, pressed them into her skin, and waited until she gave up a throaty moan of carnal delight. Then he withdrew and regarded Alerice.

"Look at me, pretty thing," he said in a voice so clear that Alerice knew she was his to command. "How do you find me?"

"You..." How Alerice found her voice, she had no idea. "You leave me speechless, sir."

"Clearly not," he said with a grin, at which point small shoots of flame danced about the corners of his lips. Sukaar paused to examine Alerice, and a moment passed before a hint of fire flashed across his black eyes. "A Realme Walker. I can see why my wife, Imari, Mother of Water and Wind, has decreed that you should be honored. You are indeed rare."

Sukaar held Alerice in his sights a moment longer before he turned to Allya. "So, my beloved. Why have you summoned me? Or rather, why did this sweet thing ask you to?"

Allya regarded her god and lover, and then her guest. "Alerice?"

Alerice knew it was her moment to stand up and make her case, but the initial inertia presented quite a barrier.

"Great God--" she began.

"You may address me directly," Sukaar said.

Alerice forced herself to nod sharply. "Sukaar, Father Fire. I ask for your help. As... you see and know," she said, gesturing to her black scale mail, "I serve the Raven Queen, but she and the king have begun to contest one another."

"When don't they?" Sukaar replied.

Alerice was not certain how to respond, and looked at Allya for guidance. However, Allya simply smiled and gestured that she should continue.

Alerice screwed up what courage she could and said, "Father Fire, I wish to settle things between them before they fall victim to their own shortsightedness and cause the Evherealme lasting damage."

"Why?"

"...Sir?"

"Why do you concern yourself with those two? You are mortal. They are everlasting. Do you believe they will heed anything you say?"

Alerice decided it was best to press her case as she had to the Raven Queen about the wizard and the Wyld.

"Sir, I have no idea if I will be successful. In truth, I may likely fail, and I may fail to persuade you to aid me. However, I have made up my mind to try, and I believe that with..."

She wasn't certain if she should continue her present thought, but she could see Sukaar waiting for her words, and so she said, "With the presence of an immortal father behind me, I might make those two see sense."

Sukaar looked Alerice over, then regarded Allya. Allya shrugged her shoulders with an 'It's true' expression, and Sukaar returned his attention to Alerice.

"Have you always been this straightforward?"

"Great God, when it comes to solving problems, I--"

"It was a comment, girl. I can see your entire life as I look at you."

"Of course you can, Father Fire," Alerice said with enough personal fortitude that Sukaar seemed to respect it.

Sukaar drew a step closer to Alerice, his presence taking hold of her as might a lord taking the leash of his hound. "My beloved Allya told you that there would be a price in summoning me, yes?"

"Yes, sir," Alerice said, trembling with a sensation not born of fear.

"Whether I aid you or no?" he asked, drawing closer.

"Um hmm," she managed to say, forbidding herself to move.

Sukaar stepped before Alerice and reached to her blonde hair. Wispy redness floated out from his fingertips, singeing it. She could smell the pungent odor even as he smiled as would a lover about to take a woman to his bed.

"I will aid you, Alerice Linden, Walker of the Evherealme. And the price shall be a kiss."

Sukaar took Alerice by the left side of her neck. His touch torched her hair and burned her skin. Alerice fought back her voice as he drew her close and kissed her cheek.

His power filled her even as his heat assaulted her.

His kiss was as passionate as it was painful. Alerice could feel her skin crinkle and blister below his lips, and yet she felt the rush of his power fill her toe to top, enlivening her as she never thought any man could.

***

Souls flew into the Hall of Eternity. The King of Shadows stood within the center of the glyph-inscribed floor, holding the Queen's Eye. He raised his head, closing his dark gray eyes as he commanded the souls fly to him. He ordered them to enter his body, savoring each as he might a delicacy.

He soon reached his fill and stood silently, his grip tightening on the Eye. The souls flitted and circled above. With a sweep of his free hand, he chased them all from the hall so that they flew past the columns and the statues of fighting men and women of arts.

The Raven Queen sat upon her throne, her Raven Knights standing behind her. She stared forward, her amethyst eyes displaying no sign that she was cogent.

The maiden Oddwyn stood nearer to the queen than she might normally. She knew that the queen had deliberately detached herself from the moment, for she always took the measure of souls before placing them. The king's disregard for this process was something the queen could not abide.

Oddwyn glanced past the king's throne to behold Kreston standing at the base of the dais. Her ice-blue eyes narrowed upon him, for he bore sole responsibility for this travesty. He could stand 'eyes forward' all he wished. Oddwyn knew that Kreston was well aware of what he had wrought. Hopefully, it was eating him alive.

The King of Shadows held wide his arms and let out a satisfied exhale. Then he paced up the dais' steps, twirled about so that his long open robe parted and its crystalline trim caught the light, and sat as might a satiated glutton.

He held up the Queen's Eye and gazed into its swirling interior, musing at its mesmerizing nature, then grinned as he glanced aside at the queen. She remained fixated on some distant place. Dissatisfied at her lack of response, the king set his sights on Oddwyn. He offered the herald a kiss, though he made only a slight motion with his lips. The gesture resonated, and Oddwyn nodded her reluctant acceptance.

The king sat back in his throne, his Shadow Warriors behind him. He glanced at Kreston, who, like the queen, was immobile. Annoyed that no one present would grant him the attention he craved, the king began turning the Queen's Eye about in his fingertips. However, then a distortion within the Hall of Eternity caught his attention.

It caught Oddwyn's and Kreston's attention as well, for it was forming into a portal. Yet unlike all Realme portals, which bore the signature tri-colors of black, midnight blue, and deep teal, this one was ringed in crackles of fire.

The Raven Queen regained consciousness as she sat more alert, and all watched the portal widen.

Alerice stepped through. Her unburned blonde hair bore pearl, red, and gold highlights. Her black scale mail was now tinged with gold on each plate, and the left side of her face bore a hideous yet luminescent scar, as if she had been burned.

"Alerice!" Kreston cried as he took a step forward. He began to reach out to her, but he held himself in check.

Alerice stepped forward to the dais. Her eyes were amazingly bright. She reverenced to the Raven Queen, and then turned fully to the King of Shadows.

"Give me the Eye, Your Majesty."

"What did you just say?" the king demanded, rising.

"I'm sorry, Your Majesty," Alerice said with a grin. "I did not realize that you had trouble hearing me." She turned to Oddwyn and asked, "Oddwyn, do you want to shout the response, or should I?"

Though shocked at her manner and appalled at her injury, Oddwyn could not contain a smirk. However, she snapped to attention as the King of Shadows glared at her.

The Raven Queen rose and looked down upon her champion. "You bear his kiss."

"Indeed, she does," Sukaar said as he sauntered forward from the portal, which ignited into a full conflagration as he passed. "For I am here to help her with her task," he said to the king.

Alerice held out her hand. "Your Majesty?"

"I do not take orders from you," the king snapped.

"Of course you don't, you petty ghost," Sukaar said. "But you should, and while you might not listen to her, you both *will* listen to me!"

In a flash of flame, Sukaar transformed into a great golden serpent. His scales shone in opalescent hues that gave off red wisps. His body coiled about the Hall of Eternity, and he drew the dais, its thrones, and their occupants, to him in his coils as his giant diamond head hovered over theirs.

"Get away, Herald," Sukaar ordered Oddwyn.

Oddwyn did not need to be told a second time as she hurried to the side of the hall.

"This is not your domain, Sukaar," the King of Shadows protested.

"Shade, it never ceases to amaze me that you are so willing to state the obvious."

"Then why are you here?" the Raven Queen asked.

"Because of this child," he replied, his gaze bearing down on the Realme's rulers. "Alerice can see what you cannot, that you two have again set yourselves on a course that will only end in your reduction.

"You," he said to the queen. "You created a trinket that gave you too much control over the Evherealme. Your husband was bound to covet it. And you," he said to the king. "You took it like some petty thief. Now give the Eye to Alerice, for if anyone knows what to do with it, she does. She bears my fire, so challenge her at your own risk. She may not be able to stand the test of immortality against you, but she can diminish you."

The King of Shadows held up the Queen's Eye, then glared from under his brow at Sukaar.

Sukaar drew a breath and bellowed fire upon the dark couple. Kreston bolted away for his own safety. Alerice, however, held her ground, for the fire did not injure her.

The king and queen both recoiled at the blast, and then recovered. The king reluctantly held out the Eye, which the queen caused to float into Alerice's grasp.

Alerice smiled as she took the gem. She held it up before the two rulers, and then conjured fire to engulf it, burning it red hot. Its outer crystalline casing cracked, and the gray swirl within began to leach out. Alerice concentrated on the Eye a moment more, and then hurled it against the hall's floor where it shattered into a thousand shards.

Sukaar returned to his mortal guise, his red velvets trimmed in gold alive with power. He beckoned for Alerice to turn to him so that he might touch her scarred cheek.

"Alerice Linden, I give you a choice. Come with me and serve as Allya's devotee, or remain here with these two unworthy specters and serve the Realme. You shall remain a Walker either way, only in my service you shall be more than these two deserve. My wife, Imari, has decreed that Walkers should be prized, but I can see that you..." Sukaar also tilted his head in Kreston's direction. "That you have not been. Not as greatly as you should have been, in any case."

Alerice nuzzled against the god's hand and smiled. Then she withdrew and stood back.

"Father Fire, Great God and Lover, I will stay and serve the Realme. I was born to be its Walker, and I belong in the shadows."

Sukaar nodded, accepting her choice. He then gazed at the king and queen, imposing the full force of his being over them.

"I give you permission to remove my kiss and take her fire, though she is perhaps foolish after all to give it away. However, I will look in upon her from time to time. I will also seal the Evherealme from further breaches. Should anyone attempt to bring more forth..." he said, looking at the King of Shadows, "I will know of it."

The Realme's rulers said nothing as Sukaar turned and created another fiery portal. He strode toward it, not glancing back, and sealed it behind himself as he left.

Alerice watched it dissolve, and then turned to the dais. She took a knee before the king and queen, and looked up into their joined gaze.

The King of Shadows and the Raven Queen descended to her. They reached out together and touched her face. Extending their combined essence, they pressed fingertips against her curdled cheek and drew out all traces of Sukaar's vitality.

Her scar vanished, except for a trail along her jaw, and her blonde hair lost most of its highlights. Her damaged hair grew back to full length, and Alerice closed her eyes as the Realme's cool power filled her.

The king and queen withdrew, ascended the dais, and sat together upon their thrones.

Alerice rose and reverenced to them, sincerity in her deference. Then she glanced at Kreston before addressing the king.

"Your Majesty, I wish to speak with Captain Dühalde. May I have your leave to bring him back into Mortalia?"

The king offered a dismissive wave of his hand. The queen followed by creating a portal in the Hall's center.

Alerice turned to the man she sought. "Kreston?"

He advanced. Alerice joined him, and they walked abreast into the portal.

***

Kreston watched as Alerice skipped a pebble across the little lake below Allya's tower. The stone basin showed no signs of the kelpie battle. The flame spouts fired and spurted. The lush vines dotted with burgundy blooms swayed gently in the breeze.

She bent down to fetch another pebble, but Kreston was quicker to pick one up. He handed it over, and she smiled before she took it and skipped it across the lake.

"One question," he said.

"Only one?" she asked.

"Alerice, I've learned not to ask too many questions when people do things that are clearly insane."

"Is that what I did?"

"Yes. Not only were you free of them, you had power over them. And you gave it up? That is clearly insane."

"But I didn't want the power, Kreston. Sukaar is a demanding master. His life wasn't right for me." Kreston tsked his disapproval, and so Alerice continued with, "So what was your question?"

Kreston paused and then asked, "Why did you show them any respect? The king and queen?"

"Because they deserved it."

"No, they didn't."

"Yes, they did, Kreston. You said it yourself. They are eternal. You and I are merely dots. I'd say that's worth a little respect."

Kreston had no reply. He picked up his own stone and was about to skip it across the water, but he dropped it on the sandy shore.

"Alerice, why did you do it? Why did you maim yourself?"

"It wasn't my first choice," she said.

"No, but it was the choice you pursued. Why sacrifice yourself for them?"

"I didn't do it for them. I did it for the Realme. Perhaps I even did it for myself, just as you used me against the queen for yourself."

Kreston closed his hazel eyes and sighed. "I am so sorry for that, Alerice. I can't tell you how much."

"Kreston, look at me." He did, and she continued. "I forgive you. I understand that you did what you did because you were trying once more to escape. I see now that you are a prisoner, and you are desperate for freedom. I would be too."

He gazed upon her, took her by the shoulders, and brushed back a lock of her blonde hair.

"But, your face, Alerice. Your lovely face."

"I still have it, just with a little scar to remind me. You must have scars to remind you of what you've done."

"Plenty, but I deserved each of them. You didn't. You did not come to the Realme of your own accord. I did. I sought the king's power, and he gave it to me. You? You were innocent."

"Perhaps I was once, but no longer. I'm keeping the armor, Kreston. I'm keeping my place at the Raven Queen's side, but I am not going to rest until I find some way to free you. I don't know why you wanted the king's power, and it honestly doesn't matter. I don't think that you intended to become his slave, and perhaps if you had known this would be your fate, you might not have sought him out.

"The Raven Queen would allow me to leave if I ever grew that discontented with her, but the king is obviously a much harder master, and that's not right. And you know how I set my mind to fixing things that aren't right."

Kreston smirked. His common retort would be self-admonishment. He had sought the King of Shadows because of what had happened to his brigade and his brothers in arms. He had sought to take revenge upon the commander who had betrayed him.

However, as he looked at her, he could not help but think that perhaps, and how, he had no idea, but perhaps she might be able to do what she intended. She might be able to help him find a way out of bondage and to atone for the crimes he had committed.

He pulled her to him, and she did not resist. There was nothing else to do but believe in her. Which made their kiss all the more sweet.

Tales of the Ravensdaughter
will continue with
Adventure Five
Mistress of Her Own Game

PLEASE REVIEW THIS BOOK:

If you enjoyed **Rips in the Ether**, please leave a review.

AMAZON

GOODREADS

AUTHOR'S WEBSITE

Thank you and blessings,
Erin Hunt Rado
ErinRadoAuthor.com

BOOKS IN THIS SERIES

Tales of the Ravensdaughter - Collection One

The Beast Of Basque

The Thief Of Souls

The Wizard And The Wyld

Rips In The Ether

Mistress Of Her Own Game

The Raven's Daughter

Made in the USA
Columbia, SC
18 October 2022